Brianna
the Bee Fairy

Join the **Rainbow Magic Reading Challenge!**

Read the story and collect your fairy points to climb the

Rea

To Faith Hills, who loves the fairies

Special thanks to
Rachel Elliot

ORCHARD BOOKS

First published in Great Britain in 2020 by The Watts Publishing Group

1 3 5 7 9 10 8 6 4 2

A CIP catalogue record for this book is available from the British Library.

ISBN 978 1 40836 318 8

Printed and bound in Great Britain by Clays Ltd, Elcograf S.p.A

MIX
Paper from
responsible sources
FSC® C104740
www.fsc.org

The paper and board used in this book are made from wood from responsible sources

Orchard Books
An imprint of Hachette Children's Group
Part of The Watts Publishing Group Limited
Carmelite House, 50 Victoria Embankment, London EC4Y 0DZ

An Hachette UK Company
www.hachette.co.uk
www.hachettechildrens.co.uk

Brianna
the Bee Fairy

By Daisy Meadows

ORCHARD

www.rainbowmagicbooks.co.uk

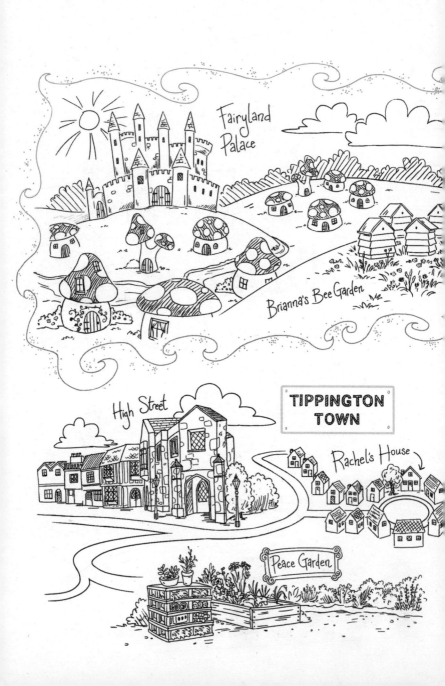

Jack Frost's
Ice Castle

↖ Goblin
Circus Tent

WETHERBURY

← Wetherbury
Market

Mr. Clover's
Bee Garden ↙

Contents

Story One:

The Buzzing Bottle

Story Two:
The Beehive Bracelet

Story Three:
The Pollen Packet

Jack Frost's Spell

A pesky bee has stung my nose!
It's sore and redder than a rose.
Brianna's friends must face the cost
Of damaging the great Jack Frost!

With magic charms at their command
My goblins have the upper hand.
From today the bees will find
They are unloved by humankind!

Story One
The Buzzing Bottle

Chapter One
A Disappointing Start

"There," said Kirsty Tate, putting the last badge into her rucksack and zipping it up. "I've made fifteen Bee Kind badges."

"Me too," said her best friend, Rachel Walker. "That makes thirty altogether. We had twenty-two phone calls about the club, so there should be plenty of

badges for everyone."

The girls shared a happy smile.

"Isn't it exciting that so many people like our idea?" said Kirsty. "Hopefully they will all spread the message that the bees need our help."

Kirsty was staying in Tippington with Rachel for the first week of the summer holiday. After working on the Tippington peace garden, they had realised how much they enjoyed doing things for the community. When they found out that bees were disappearing from the world, they decided to start a club – Bee Kind – to teach people how to help save the bees. Today was the first meeting. They were starting by placing a water basin in the peace garden, surrounded by bee-friendly flowers.

"Have we got everything we'll need?" asked Rachel.

"Water bottles, badges and the water basin," said Kirsty.

"I've got the sun cream, the seeds and the camera," said Rachel. "Let's go!"

It didn't take them long to walk to the peace garden. The iron entrance gate had been made specially by the local blacksmith with curving tendrils, leaves and flowers. They pushed it open and walked in.

The peace garden was always a quiet place, but this morning there was no one else there. Brightly coloured flowers nodded in the breeze, and the only sound was the faint tinkle of wind chimes. Marnie, the head gardener, had set aside a flowerbed near the gate for the girls to do their planting.

"Oh look, Marnie's left out lots of gardening tools and watering cans for us," said Rachel, slipping her rucksack off her bag. "How kind."

"People should start arriving any

minute," said Kirsty, who was keeping an eye on the gate.

"Lots of my friends from school said they'd come along," said Rachel.

They sat cross-legged by the flowerbed and waited . . . and waited . . . and waited. The sun rose higher in the sky. The distant hum of Tippington traffic grew louder. But no one came through the iron gate. A horrible, disappointed

feeling crept over both girls.

"I don't understand," said Kirsty. "Could we have written the time wrong on the posters?"

"No, we checked them about ten times before we put them up," Rachel replied.

"Maybe they're waiting outside the gate," Kirsty suggested.

They went down to the gate, but no one was waiting there. Then a couple of teenage girls came strolling along the pavement arm in arm.

"Are you here for the Bee Kind club?" Rachel blurted out.

The girls stopped in surprise and shook their heads.

"Would you like to come?" asked Kirsty. "It's to help the bees."

"Bees?" repeated one of the girls with a

giggle. "Who cares about bees?"

Laughing, the girls carried on walking.

"Why wouldn't people care about bees?" asked Rachel, confused.

"Because of Jack Frost," said a tinkling

voice behind them.

Rachel and Kirsty whirled around and gasped. A tiny fairy was sitting in one of the gate's iron tendrils.

Chapter Two
The Bee Garden

"Hi," said the fairy with a little wave. "I'm Brianna the Bee Fairy."

She was wearing a loose-fitting yellow T-shirt with blue shorts and a pair of sandals. A yellow scrunchie held back her hair, and her gauzy wings were as blue as the summer sky.

"Hi, Brianna," said Kirsty. "It's lovely to meet you, but what do you mean about Jack Frost? Why would he want to spoil our club?"

"He wants to spoil anything to do with bees," said Brianna with a sigh. "That's why I'm here. Will you come with me to the Fairyland Bee Garden? I really need your help."

"Of course we'll come," said Rachel at once.

Brianna waved her wand, sprinkling the girls with yellow fairy dust that glittered and flashed in the sunlight. They felt themselves shrinking, and wings sprang from their shoulders. They each felt a rush of sudden gladness. Becoming a fairy was the best feeling they knew. They fluttered up to Brianna.

"Follow me," she said.

Brianna darted through an iron spiral in the entrance gate . . . and vanished.

Rachel and Kirsty exchanged a confused glance. How could this ordinary gate lead to another world?

"Let's go together," said Kirsty, feeling a tingle of excitement down her spine.

Hand in hand, they flew towards the spiral. As they reached it, the air shimmered, and they felt a wave of warmth ripple over them. Then they found themselves standing in a small, flowery meadow.

"Welcome to my Bee Garden," said Brianna.

Wooden beehives were dotted around the meadow, and a pleasant buzzing sound filled the air.

"What a lovely place," said Rachel.

"Thanks," said Brianna. "But it's already in danger. The water basins have disappeared, the bees have stopped making honey and the flowers are dying.

Just look."

In a corner of the meadow, the grass had gone brown and flowers had withered.

"It's only been like that since this morning," Brianna said.

"What happened this morning?"
Rachel asked.

"I had an open morning for anyone
who wanted to learn about bees," said
Brianna. "I arranged a special guest and
I planned to show everyone how to care
for bees."

"Just like our club," said Kirsty.

"Yes," said Brianna. "I even made a
display with all my magical objects. But
the first visitors were Jack Frost and three
of his goblins."

"What happened?" asked Rachel.

"Jack Frost was making fun of
everything," said Brianna. "He started
sneering at the flowers in the meadow,
saying they were ugly and had no smell.
He bent down to sniff one, and his
pointy nose poked a worker bee who was

collecting pollen. The worker bee was really scared, and it stung him."

"Oh no," said Kirsty, putting her hand to her mouth.

"Jack Frost was furious," said Brianna. "His nose swelled up and went bright red. He shouted and shouted, and all the bees were terrified. Then he snatched my magical objects and said that he would punish all bees, here and in the human world. I couldn't stop him."

"Let's go to the Ice Castle right now," said Rachel. "We'll find your magical objects and bring them home."

"There's something else," said Brianna. "My special guest was an old friend of yours – Queenie the Queen Bee."

"Oh, brilliant," said Kirsty, looking around. "We haven't seen her since our

adventure with Rosie the Honey Bear
Fairy. Where is she?"

"That's just it," said Brianna in a
small voice. "After Jack Frost and the

goblins left, I realised that they had taken Queenie with them. She's been bee-napped!"

Chapter Three
Truce!

As the fairies zoomed across Fairyland towards Jack Frost's castle, Brianna told them about the things that had been stolen.

"The buzzing bottle is a reusable water bottle that reminds people to leave dishes of water out for bees in hot weather," she said. "The beehive bracelet encourages everyone to buy local honey, and the pollen packet inspires people to plant wildflowers in their gardens for bees to pollinate."

"Do you know what Jack Frost is going to do with them?" asked Rachel.

"No, but while he has them, their magic will be working for him and not for me," said Brianna. "Humans will forget all about helping bees. Without bees to pollinate plants, the human world will lose many of its crops, and there won't be enough food. Everyone will suffer."

"That's terrible," said Kirsty. "We have to get your magical objects back quickly – and save Queenie."

The Ice Castle loomed up in front of

them. Its turrets were thick with icicles, and it looked even colder and scarier than ever. A goblin guard was leaning against the oak door. He spotted them and started pointing and shouting.

"What are we going to do?" cried Brianna.

"I have an idea," said Rachel. "Maybe we can do this another way. Brianna, can you make me a white flag?"

Brianna waved her wand and a white flag appeared in Rachel's hand, fluttering in the frosty air. The fairies landed in front of the goblin guard.

"Clear off!" he squawked, flapping his hands.

Rachel stepped forward.

"Do you know what this flag means?" she asked the goblin.

He shook his head.

"It's a sign of peace," said Rachel. "People wave one when they want a truce and a talk without tricks. Please tell Jack Frost that we have come with a white flag and we want to talk."

The goblin's mouth hung open in astonishment. He reached behind him, opened the door and backed through it. The door slammed shut.

"Do you think he's going to let us in?" Kirsty asked.

Rachel shrugged and crossed her fingers. They waited in silence. The icy wind whistled around the castle. Then the door creaked open and a green hand

appeared. One bony
finger beckoned
them in.

"Shall we go?"
asked Brianna.

"We must," said
Rachel. "We are
Queenie's only hope."

The goblin guard led the fairies along a
dark, damp corridor. As they went, more
goblins scurried past, darting suspicious
glances at them. They followed the guard
up a long, spiral staircase. Kirsty thought
that she recognised it.

"I think this leads to Jack Frost's
bedroom," she whispered to Rachel.

"I think you're right," Rachel whispered
back. "We've been here before."

Brianna shuddered – partly because

of the cold and partly at the thought of seeing Jack Frost again. Kirsty squeezed her hand.

"We're all in this together," she said. "We're the Bee Team! We can do this."

Chapter Four
A Sore Nose

At the top of the staircase was a single wooden door. There was a lightning bolt painted on it, with the initials JF in the centre. The goblin pushed open the door and bowed.

"The pests with their – er – flag thing, Your Iciness," he mumbled.

The fairies stepped through the door.
Rachel and Kirsty had seen Jack Frost's
bedroom before, but it had changed. A
huge mirror took up one entire wall.
On the other were hundreds of framed
photographs of Jack Frost. There was a
four-poster bed in the centre of the room,
and Jack Frost was lying in the middle of
it, propped up by pillows. He was pressing
a large ice cube against the tip of his
nose.

"What do you pesky pests want?" he
yelled at Rachel and Kirsty, and then he
saw Brianna. "And you! I never want to
see you again. Look at my nose!"

He removed the ice cube for a moment.
His hooked nose was red and throbbing.

"I'm sorry you got stung," said Brianna.
"But the bee was scared."

"It's not fair to punish the bees," Kirsty added. "Without Brianna's magical objects, there is nothing to protect bees in the human world."

"Who cares?" said Jack Frost.

"Humans have been careless for years, and their actions have put bees in danger," exclaimed Brianna, her cheeks flushing. "Without my magic, their habitats will vanish and they will disappear from the world. Then humans will be in danger too. Please change your mind and give me back what's mine."

Jack Frost stared at her.

"Are you telling me that if I harm the bees, then humans will suffer too?" he asked.

"Yes," said Brianna, relieved that he understood at last.

A nasty grin spread over Jack Frost's face.

"That's the best thing I've heard all day," he hissed. "Bees die? Good! Humans suffer? Good! Now leave me alone."

Rachel and Kirsty exchanged a
desperate glance.

"You're just being mean because you're
hurt," said Rachel. "I know you're not
that unkind."

"Even if I wanted to help you, which I don't, I couldn't," said Jack Frost. "I've given everything I took to the goblins, and I don't know or care where they are, as long as they're not in my castle."

"I bet they've gone to Goblin Grotto," said Kirsty. "It's not far away."

She and Rachel turned to leave, but Brianna hesitated. Then she waved her wand and a single, shining sparkle of fairy dust landed on Jack Frost's red nose. Instantly, the swelling went down and the redness disappeared.

"That's the least you could do," was all Jack Frost said.

The fairies hurried out of the room and back down the spiral staircase, feeling more worried than ever. If Queenie and the magical objects were in the heart of

the goblin village, there was no telling what might have happened to them.

It didn't take long for the fairies to reach Goblin Grotto. The village lay at the foot of a snowy hill, crammed with higgledy-piggledy wooden huts.

"Where do we start?" asked Brianna. "The objects could be anywhere."

"I've never seen that before," said

Rachel, pointing at a yellow-and-black stripy tent in the centre of the village. "That's where the goblins put their tree at Christmas."

They flew closer and saw crowds of goblins milling around the tent. There was a sign on a blackboard outside.

"That must be Queenie," said Kirsty, feeling sick with worry. "Oh my goodness, we can't let them tie up her wings!"

Chapter Five
Stinky Feet

"There are two hours to go before the show," said Brianna. "If we can get my magical objects back before then, I'll have enough magic to rescue Queenie."

"We have to search," said Rachel. "But the goblins will spot us straight away."

With a beaming smile, Brianna waved

her wand and gave each of them a thick cloak.

"This will disguise us and keep us warm," she said.

Their hearts thumping, the three fairies joined the crowd of goblins. There were a few hastily made stalls around the tent, selling some of the goblins' favourite foods. Kirsty spotted bogmallows, frosty fungus jelly beans and green sherbet sweets. There was a goblin painting faces using a red crayon, and another drawing portraits that all looked like stick people. One goblin was trying to make balloon animals, but the balloons kept popping and scaring him.

"Magic foot wash?" squawked a goblin crouching on the ground beside them.

The fairies hurriedly hid their feet under their cloaks, and the goblin squinted up at them.

"Er, no thanks," said Kirsty in her gruffest voice.

"Oh, go on," said the goblin. "You know that goblin feet are super-stinky and need to be washed every year. My magic foot-washing bottle can get all the cheesy toe fluff out. It never runs out of water."

"That's OK, our feet already smell

great," said Brianna.

"Fine," snapped the goblin in a sulky voice. "Are you scared because my water bottle buzzes? It still works, you know."

Rachel and Kirsty exchanged an excited glance.

"Did you say it buzzes?" Rachel asked.

"Yes, stupid thing," said the goblin.
"I expect it's got some wires crossed
inside. Just my luck to get the worst
present from Jack Frost. No one is
coming to me for a foot wash."

He took out a blue water bottle with
a purple lid. It glowed faintly, and there
were two sparkling silver drops of water
painted on its side. The whole thing made
a low buzzing sound. It sounded like a
far-off colony of bees.

"That's it," Brianna whispered. "That's
my buzzing bottle."

"I have an idea," said Kirsty.

She knelt down beside the grumpy
goblin.

"Would you like a really special water
bottle?" she asked. "We could swap this
noisy one for a sparkly green one that

doesn't buzz."

The goblin looked very excited.

"Yes please," he said at once. "Then I might actually get some customers."

Under the cover of her cloak, Brianna waved her wand. There was a faint green flash, and then she held out a bottle to the goblin. It was pale green with a dark green lid, and it seemed to be filled with glowing green fairy lights. A picture of the goblin was painted in silver on the side of the bottle.

"Ohhh," whispered the goblin. "That's the best I've ever seen."

He pushed the buzzing bottle into
Kirsty's hands and snatched the new one
from Brianna. He tipped it up, and green
water flowed out.

"Perfect," he said.

The fairies turned away and shared a
happy hug.

"Thank you both," said Brianna. "I
can't believe we've found it."

"The beehive bracelet and the pollen packet must be nearby," said Kirsty. "Let's keep looking. We have to rescue Queenie before the show starts at twelve o'clock!"

Story Two
The Beehive Bracelet

Chapter Six
Fairies at the Food Fair

Rachel, Kirsty and Brianna ducked behind the yellow-and-black stripy tent to catch their breath. Brianna tucked the buzzing bottle into the pocket of her cloak.

"Oh my goodness, that was scary," she said, putting her hand over her heart. "I never imagined that I would be in the heart of the goblin village today."

Just then, they heard goblins squabbling nearby.

"Why did you give it away?" a shrill voice demanded. "You idiot! That was one of those magical fairy thingummybobs Jack Frost gave us."

Magic Foot Wash

"I don't care," said the goblin they had met earlier. "I love my new water bottle and I'm keeping it, so there."

He blew a loud raspberry.

"I'm keeping mine," said the shrill-voiced goblin. "It's helping me at the Wetherbury market today."

They heard the goblins move away. The fairies exchanged alarmed glances.

"Wetherbury is where I live," Kirsty told Brianna. "My mum told me about a food fair in the village today. That must be where the goblin is going. But why?"

"I'll magic us there so that we can find out," said Brianna, raising her wand.

"Let's stay as fairies," said Kirsty. "If my parents see us in Wetherbury when we're supposed to be in Tippington, I won't know how to explain."

Brianna nodded, and waved her wand. A flurry of yellow sparkles whooshed around them and clung to their hair, making them glow with fairy dust. The next moment, they were fluttering above Wetherbury in the sunshine. Their cloaks had disappeared. The busy high street was lined with stalls, decorated with colourful cloth bunting. There were banners advertising freshly laid eggs, local butter, rustic bread and homemade pies.

"Everything smells so good," said Rachel. "It's making my tummy rumble."

"Can you see the goblins?" Brianna asked.

They fluttered lower, scanning the crowds for any sign of a goblin.

"Look, there's a honey stall," said Rachel in excitement.

Under a bee-shaped flag, which said 'Wetherbury Honey', was a stall selling neatly stacked glass jars. Each one was filled with golden, runny honey. Some of them even had honeycombs inside.

"Yum, they look so sticky and

delicious," said Kirsty. "I hope my mum buys some."

A rosy-faced man was standing behind the table, looking around eagerly. His stall was the only one without any customers.

"That's Mr Clover," said Brianna. "He looks after the Wetherbury Bee Garden."

"Do you know all the beekeepers in the world?" Rachel asked.

Brianna nodded.

"Local beekeepers like Mr Clover depend on selling lots of honey at food fairs like this," she said. "When people buy local honey, they help to make sure that the beekeepers can keep caring for their bees."

The fairies fluttered further along the high street, glancing into each stall and watching out for goblins. A little further along, there was a large crowd around a green stripy stall.

"I can't see what they're selling," said Rachel.

The fairies dared to flutter a little closer,

and Kirsty gasped.

"There's my mum," she said in an excited voice. "I wish I could go and give her a hug. But it would be too hard

to try to explain how we are here in Wetherbury when we are supposed to be in Tippington."

The crowd parted for a moment, and the fairies glimpsed a higgledy-piggledy pile of jars with something green inside. They exchanged worried glances.

"Green equals goblins," Rachel exclaimed. "What are we going to do now?"

Chapter Seven
Green Honey

A squawking voice shouted above the hum of the crowd.

"Get your local honey here!" they cried. "Delicious honey straight from the best bees!"

Rachel, Kirsty and Brianna exchanged surprised looks.

"But the goblins don't know how to make honey," said Brianna. "And I'm sure they don't have any bees."

A few people walked away from the stall, each holding a jar. From above, the fairies couldn't see what was inside.

"Let's fly around to the back," Kirsty suggested.

Hovering behind the stall, they saw two boys serving the customers. They were wearing green jumpers, knitted beanie hats and baggy trousers.

"Are they goblins?" Brianna whispered.

Rachel and Kirsty nodded.

"Look at their big feet," said Rachel in a low voice. "It's hard for goblins to disguise those."

"Have you seen the honey jars they're selling?" asked Kirsty.

The jars were filled with what looked like green slime. Brianna wrinkled up her nose.

"That doesn't look like honey," she said.

"Why is everyone buying it?" asked Rachel. "It looks horrible."

"It's because the goblins have my

magical bracelet," Brianna explained. "It makes people want to buy local honey and support their local bee gardens. They're using all the magic, so it doesn't matter what they're selling. As long as it's labelled 'honey', the magic will encourage people to buy it."

"That's not fair," said Rachel, glancing at the Wetherbury Honey stall. "The Wetherbury bees have worked hard to make that honey and now nobody is buying it."

Brianna looked worried.

"Yes," she said. "It's important for us to get the bracelet back as quickly as we can – for bees, for Queenie and for beekeepers all around the world."

Just then, the taller goblin rolled up his sleeves, and all three fairies noticed a yellow bracelet tied around his wrist. It was pattered with delicate hexagon shapes like a honeycomb, and it glowed as if it were made of sunshine.

"That must be your bracelet," Kirsty said.

Brianna nodded, and her eyes sparkled.

"Isn't it beautiful?" she said.

"It looks as if he has tied it on tightly," said Rachel. "It's not going to be easy to get it back."

"I wish we could stop people from buying any more," said Brianna. "I'm sure that green stuff doesn't taste anything like honey."

"I've got an idea," said Kirsty. "Could you use your magic to open the lids? Maybe if the jars are open, someone might try a little bit. If it's yucky, people might stop buying it."

Brianna swished her wand and nodded.

"It's done," she said. "I made the lids

fall off all the jars that have already been sold."

Rachel and Kirsty crossed their fingers. "Please let it work," Rachel whispered.

Chapter Eight
Mr Clover's Field

"Excuse me," called a voice from the crowd. "This doesn't taste right."

"I want my money back," called another voice. "There's something wrong with my honey."

"Go away," the taller goblin yelled.

"It's not honey," said a white-haired

lady, holding up her open jar. "It smells like moss."

"Ungrateful!" shouted the shorter goblin. "We made it with the best bogmallows."

More voices started to complain, and the goblins backed away from the stall.

"I know where we can get some different honey to sell," said the shorter

goblin. "Come on!"

"Follow them!" exclaimed Kirsty.

The goblins ran down the high street and darted down the lane beside the sweet shop. The fairies zoomed after them, up the hill towards Greenwood Forest. But instead of going into the forest, they clambered over a stile and ran across a small field.

"I've never been this way before," said Kirsty.

"This land belongs to Mr Clover," said Brianna. "His bee garden is on the other side of the field."

Rachel and Kirsty could see five white beehives in a row beside the hedge. A few metres away was a stone cottage next to a ramshackle old shed.

"What are they planning?" Kirsty

asked Brianna.

"I don't know," said Brianna. "But it's my job to protect the bees, even without

my special objects. I just hope that the buzzing bottle gives me enough magic."

The goblins were almost at the beehives when they swerved sideways towards Mr Clover's house.

"I'll stay here and do a spell to protect the beehives," called Brianna. "You follow the goblins."

The best friends swooped after the goblins. They had already reached the

shed beside the house.

"This is where the old man got his jars of honey," said the smaller goblin.

They pushed the door open and barged in. The fairies slipped in too.

"Oh my goodness, I can't see anything,"

said Rachel.

Their eyes got used to the dim light, and they saw that the walls were lined with shelves. There were empty jars of all shapes and sizes, beekeeper's outfits hanging on hooks and a sweet smell in the air. Rachel and Kirsty held hands and perched on the highest shelf. The goblins were rummaging through the jars.

CLINK! CHINK!

"It's not fair," squawked the taller goblin, stamping his feet. "They're empty. That greedy old man must have taken all the honey to sell at the market."

"It doesn't matter," said the smaller goblin. "We can just take some of these empty jars and fill them up with the honey from the beehives."

The goblins started scooping jars into their arms.

"They've not even taken the special beekeeping outfits," said Rachel. "They're going to get stung."

"Let's warn Brianna," said Kirsty. "We don't want the goblins to be stung or the bees to be scared."

The goblins set off for the beehives, but balancing all the jars slowed them down. Rachel and Kirsty zoomed ahead of them.

"There's Brianna, on top of the third beehive," Rachel exclaimed. "Wow, look, the first three hives are glowing."

"There are still two to protect," said Kirsty with a gasp. "And the goblins are almost there!"

Chapter Nine
The Fifth Beehive

As they reached Brianna, she pointed her wand at the fourth beehive and said the words of a spell. A sparkling, golden mist poured out of her wand tip and swirled around the beehive.

"Just one more to go," said Brianna. "It's taking longer than I thought. Doing these spells without my magical objects is hard."

"The goblins are planning to steal the honey and sell it," said Kirsty. "Will your magic stop them from reaching the bees?"

"Yes, it will be just like enchanted armour," said Brianna. "The goblins won't be able to touch the beehive."

She raised her wand, panting with tiredness. But before she could perform the spell for the fifth time . . .

"You interfering little pests!" yelled a voice.

The goblins had spotted them. They flung the glass jars onto the grass and lunged at the fairies, who dived out of the way.

"Ha!" said the taller goblin.

Roughly, he flung open the beehive and peered inside. Brianna, Rachel and Kirsty picked themselves up from the ground. They had flown away from the goblins so fast that they had shot into a pile of daisies under the hedge. A few bees rose out of the hive, buzzing angrily.

"Those are the guard bees," said Brianna. "It's their job to defend the hive."

"We can't let the goblins steal the honey," cried Kirsty.

She flew up and hovered in front of the goblins.

"Please stop," she said. "This honey doesn't belong to you. The bees work hard to make it, and they share it with Mr Clover."

"Shut up," said the taller goblin.

"They've done all the hard work, now we can have the fun of selling the honey."

"You're scaring the bees, and you don't know how to take honey safely," said Brianna. "You'll be stung."

The smaller goblin backed away from the beehive.

"What are you doing?" asked the taller goblin.

"I don't want to get hurt," said the smaller goblin. "I was stung on the bottom once when I was little. It was really ouchy."

"Cowardy cowardy custard," said the taller goblin, peering into the beehive and licking his lips. "I can see honey and nectar and pollen. Yum! We'll sell it all and make lots of money. Then we can buy a proper cage for the bee circus."

The fairies exchanged worried glances as he put his hand on one of the frames, and the buzz of the guard bees grew louder. Poor Queenie was still trapped in the bee circus, and Brianna wouldn't  be able to free her without her other two magical objects.

"I can't do the spell if the goblins are touching the beehive," said Brianna. "They will be inside the armour."

"We have to move them away from the beehive," said Rachel. "But how?"

It was too late. The goblin yanked the frame out of the beehive and Brianna gasped.

"That's too rough," she exclaimed. "You could crush the bees or roll them against each other. Slow down!"

The goblin stuck out his tongue and blew a huge raspberry at her. He started turning the frame over and over, looking for the thickest stores of honey. The hum of the bees inside the hive grew louder.

"They sound scared," said Rachel.

"Hold the frame up," Brianna cried out

in alarm. "Don't let it lie flat in case the nectar and babies fall out."

The goblin ignored her. Tipping the frame, he poked one long, bony finger into a hexagon filled with nectar. One alarmed guard bee zoomed forward.

"YOWCH!" squealed the goblin. "I've been stung!"

He let go of the frame!

Chapter Ten
Goblins in Trouble!

Everything seemed to happen in slow
motion. The frame tumbled towards the
ground as Rachel and Kirsty stretched
out their arms helplessly. They were much
too small to catch it! Then, out of the
corner of her eye, Kirsty saw Brianna's
wand swish. A wave of fairy dust surged

towards the frame and caught it like a net, sweeping it safely upwards and back into the beehive.

"Oh my goodness, that was so close," said Kirsty.

The goblins were scrambling away from the beehives, with a line of guard bees streaming after them.

"The bees are scared and angry," said Brianna.

"How are we going to save the goblins from more stings?" asked Kirsty.

Brianna rose into the air.

"I have an idea," she said. "Bees love music. Let's sing to them, but stay well back. It's important to give bees lots of space when they're cross."

The fairies fluttered after the guard bees, who were chasing the goblins round and round the little field.

"Leave us alone!" wailed the smaller goblin.

"My hand!" screeched the taller one.

"Lavender's blue," sang Brianna. "Lavender's green."

"When I am king, dilly dilly, you shall be queen," Rachel and Kirsty chimed in.

"Call up your men, dilly dilly,
Set them to work.
Some to the plough, dilly dilly,
Some to the cart.
Some to make hay, dilly dilly,
Some to cut corn.
While you and I, dilly dilly,
Keep ourselves warm."

As the fairies sang, the bees slowed down and their angry buzz slowly became a gentle hum.

"Come on, my friends," said Brianna in a low, sweet voice. "It's time to go back to your hive."

The bees hovered beside her for a moment, and then turned and headed back towards their home. The goblins reached the stile and the smaller one scrambled over it.

"I never want to see a bee again as

long as I live!" squawked the taller one.

He ripped the bracelet off his wrist and followed the other goblin over the stile. Rachel and Kirsty let out sighs of relief.

"Phew," said Brianna. "Those silly goblins didn't realise that bees can be dangerous when they feel scared. It's so important to treat them with kindness and respect."

Smiling, Rachel waved Brianna over to the stile. The beautiful bracelet lay in the grass, glowing like the sun. Brianna placed her hand on it, and it instantly returned to fairy size. She tied it on to her wrist.

"Thank you for helping me," she said, smiling at Rachel and Kirsty. "Now people will want to buy the Wetherbury honey again."

Kirsty had been watching the guard bees as they flew back to their home.

"Look," she said in delight. "I think they're saying thank you too."

Above their hive, the bees flew into the shape of a heart. They hovered there for a moment, and then zoomed back to guard their queen.

The Bee Fairy waved her wand, and the golden mist melted away from the other beehives.

"They're safe now," she said. "Goodbye, bees. See you soon!"

"There's just one magical object left to find," said Kirsty. "Then we can rescue Queenie."

"We have to go back to Goblin Grotto," said Brianna. "I hope that we can find the wildflower seed packet before the goblins tie up Queenie's wings and make her walk the tightrope."

"There's no time to lose," said Rachel. "Let's get back to Fairyland!"

Story Three
The Pollen Packet

Chapter Eleven
Gardening Goblins

Brianna gave her wand a little twirl, and Rachel and Kirsty were whisked into a spiral of fairy dust.

"Mmm, I can smell honey," said Kirsty, closing her eyes.

"It's like being wrapped in sparkles," said Rachel.

When the glimmering fairy dust faded, they found themselves hovering over the circus tent in the heart of the goblin village. Its yellow and black stripes were frosted with a thin layer of ice. Brianna waved her wand, and once again they were wrapped in thick cloaks. Rachel and Kirsty shared a hopeful smile. There was only one magical object left to find. As soon as they had got the pollen packet back, they could rescue Queenie.

"Where shall we start looking?" asked Brianna.

The fairies slowly turned in mid air, taking in the shabby huts and the crooked streets of Goblin Grotto. Lots of green figures were scurrying towards the circus.

"Everyone wants to see poor Queenie

walk the tightrope with her wings tied up," said Brianna. "How are we going to rescue her with every goblin watching?"

"Let's not worry about that yet," said

Rachel. "First we have to find the pollen packet. While the goblins are at the circus, it'll be easier to search the village."

"Brianna, you said that the pollen packet inspires humans to plant wildflowers in their gardens," said Kirsty. "Will it make the goblins eager to plant flowers too?"

"I think so," said Brianna. "It's not always easy to know how goblins will behave."

"Maybe we should try looking for goblin gardens," said Kirsty.

"There can't be many gardens here," said Rachel, shivering. "Not much would grow in the frost and snow."

Hand in hand, the three fairies zigzagged across the village.

"There's one!" Kirsty exclaimed,

pointing at a bare patch of earth behind a hut.

They swooped lower, but the tiny garden was empty and looked frozen solid.

"I see another," Rachel called out.

This time, the garden wasn't empty. Two goblins were kneeling there, dressed in wellies and gardening gloves, and digging with little trowels. The fairies floated down and kneeled behind a rickety old shed.

"I wonder why they haven't rushed to the circus with everyone else," said Kirsty.

"Stop digging in my patch," grumbled the bigger goblin, who had lime-green wellies.

"This ground is frozen," the other goblin complained, rubbing his red-gloved hands together. "We'll never dig deep enough to plant seeds."

"Digging is hard work," said the goblin in lime-green wellies. "Let's scatter them on the top."

He pulled a small seed packet from inside his gloves. It was glowing with a soft yellow light, and there was a picture of colourful wildflowers on the front.

"That's it," Brianna exclaimed. "My

pollen packet!"

She began to stand up, and Rachel
reached for her hand.

"Don't let them see you," she whispered.

But Brianna was longing to get her
pollen packet back, and she didn't listen.
She sprang out from behind the shed and

threw back her hood.

"I've come to take back what you stole from me," she declared. "Give back my pollen packet!"

"Fairy alert!" squawked the goblin with red gloves.

"Catch her!" yelled the other goblin.

They flung themselves at Brianna and

she dropped her wand. Rachel and Kirsty gasped as the goblins grabbed her arms tightly. Brianna was a prisoner!

Chapter Twelve
PSSST!

Kirsty swooped down and grabbed
Brianna's wand from where it had been
lying on the ground. Then she rejoined
Rachel in their hiding place.

"Oh my goodness," said Rachel, sitting
back on her heels. "This is terrible. We
have to rescue Brianna, get back the

pollen packet and save Queenie – all before the tightrope show at twelve o'clock!"

The goblins dragged Brianna into their hut and slammed the door behind her.

"Let's fetch Jack Frost," the fairies heard the goblin with the lime-green wellies say. "He'll know what to do with her."

"No, let's take her to the circus," replied the goblin with red gloves. "She can be part of the show."

"Jack Frost," squawked the first.

"Circus!" yelled the second.

"They're quarrelling," Kirsty whispered. "Let's see if we can slip in without them noticing."

They fluttered upwards and landed on the roof like falling petals. By leaning over, they could see the goblins standing next to the front door, shouting at each other.

"We have to get them away from the door," said Rachel.

"I've got an idea," said Kirsty, eagerly.

"This hut is round. If we could get the goblins to run around it a few times, they might get dizzy. We could have time to get Brianna out."

"It'll be a bit scary," said Rachel. "I hope they don't catch us!"

"We're together," said Kirsty, giving her best friend's hand a comforting squeeze. "We can do this!"

They fluttered down from the roof and

hovered at the back of the hut.

"PSSST!" they hissed as loudly as they could.

The goblins stopped shouting.

"What was that?" said the one with red gloves.

"More fairies?" said the other. "Get them!"

They raced around the hut but found nothing. Rachel and Kirsty had flown back up to the roof again. The goblins returned to the door.

"Maybe it was the wind," said the goblin in the lime-green wellies.

"PSSST!" hissed the fairies again.

"Let's try the other way," said the first goblin.

They sprinted around the hut, but again they found nothing.

"I can't understand it," said the red-gloved goblin, scratching his head. "Where is that noise coming from?"

Rachel and Kirsty had to cover their mouths to stifle their giggles. For the third time, they fluttered to the back of the hut and hissed, "PSSST!"

"Right, I'll go this way, you go that way," said the first goblin. "We'll get those pesky fairies."

They pelted around the hut and crashed into each other, bumping their knobbly heads together and falling down.

"YOWCH!" they yelled.

"Now!" whispered Kirsty.

They flew to the door of the hut and pushed it open. Brianna zoomed out, and in a few seconds they were all safely on the roof. The goblins were sitting at the

back of the hut, rubbing their sore heads and grumbling.

"They must have bumped into each other really hard," said Rachel.

"Oh my goodness," Brianna exclaimed. "They've dropped the pollen packet!"

The pollen packet was lying on the frozen ground.

"It must have fallen out when they bumped into each other," said Kirsty. "I can get it!"

Chapter Thirteen
Garden Experts

At that moment the goblin with lime-green wellies saw the packet and snatched it up.

"We can't lose that," he said. "I want my garden to be bursting with green, stinky flowers."

As the goblins stomped back to the

front door, Brianna's eyes filled up with tears.

"I can't believe it," she said. "They are going to use up all the magic of the pollen packet, and they won't even like what they get. The flowers will be every colour of the rainbow, not just green, and they will smell wonderful. Even worse, no bees will come to such a cold place, so all the precious pollen will be wasted."

"If only we could swap their seeds for ones that the goblins would like," said Kirsty.

"Maybe we can," said Rachel. "They won't listen to fairies, but they might listen to a couple of garden experts. Let's pose as garden gnomes and see if they want some new seeds."

They fluttered down to the ground and

Kirsty handed Brianna her wand. The Bee Fairy bathed them in a cascade of yellow sparkles. Instantly, their cloaks were replaced with red trousers and blue tunics that hid their wings. Each had a red, pointy hat and large brown boots.

"My chin is tickling," said Kirsty with a gasp.

Long, white beards sprouted from their chins, and bushy moustaches sprang from their upper lips.

"Oh my goodness," said Rachel, giggling. "Kirsty, I would never have recognised you!"

They each had a packet of seeds, decorated with pictures of happy goblins and green flowers.

"Good luck," whispered Brianna.

She crossed her fingers as Rachel and

Kirsty tramped around to the back of
the hut. The goblins looked startled
when they saw two gnomes coming
towards them.

"What do you want?" said the
red-gloved goblin rudely.

"We're garden experts," said Rachel in her gruffest voice. "We noticed how empty and boring goblin gardens look."

"We've got just the thing," said Kirsty, holding up her seed packet. "These will grow into the best stinky green flowers in Fairyland."

"We've already got some," said the goblin with the lime-green wellies.

He waved the pollen packet under their bulbous noses.

"Ho no," Rachel chuckled. "Those are fairy seeds. They'll be all colourful and sweet-smelling. Nice for fairies, not so nice for goblins."

"Sweet smelling?" the goblin exclaimed. "Yuck! I want seeds like yours, but I haven't got any money."

"We sometimes agree to swaps," said

Rachel. "I'm sure we could find a place for those fairy seeds."

The goblins exchanged an excited look. But then the goblin with the red gloves shook his head.

"We can't," he said. "Jack Frost told us to keep the seeds here."

"That's not exactly what he said," said the other goblin, squirming. "He only ordered us to keep them away from the fairies."

"Do we look like fairies?" said Rachel.

The goblins shook their heads. There was a long pause.

"That's OK," said Kirsty with a shrug. "I'm sure there will be other goblins who want our seeds."

She turned to leave, and Rachel followed her. They held their breath. Would the goblins let them walk away?

"Wait!" squawked the goblin with the lime-green wellies.

Chapter Fourteen
Don't Fly!

The goblin ran after them and held up the glowing pollen packet.

"Will you swap?" he said.

Smiling, Rachel and Kirsty gave him their seeds and took the pollen packet.

"Ha ha, I've got two packets," the goblin crowed. "I won!"

"Let's plant them now," said the other goblin. "We can decide what to do with that silly fairy later."

They raced back to their garden, and the garden gnomes shared a smile.

"They still think that Brianna's their prisoner," said Rachel. "They're going to be so surprised when they open the door later on."

"I don't think they'll mind," said Kirsty. "They're going to have the best garden in Goblin Grotto."

Brianna fluttered to Rachel and Kirsty from her hiding place on the other side of the hut.

"That was wonderful," she said breathlessly. "You were so brave!"

She waved her wand and, in a twinkling, Rachel and Kirsty were fairies

again. Beaming
with happiness,
Brianna took the
pollen packet and
tucked it inside her
cloak.

"My magic is
back where it
belongs," she said. "I
can put everything
right – starting with
Queenie and the
Goblin Circus."

The three fairies
flew over the
higgledy-piggledy
huts to the centre of
the goblin village.
The circus tent was

busier than ever, with goblins pouring in
to see the first performance. A goblin in

a ringmaster's hat
was standing on a
box outside the tent,
squawking at the
top of his voice.

"Roll up! Roll
up! Come and
gasp in wonder at
Buzzy the Amazing
Performing Bee.
With her wings tied
up, she will walk
the tightrope before
your very eyes!"

"Oh no she won't," said Kirsty in a
determined voice.

They floated to the ground, wrapped

in their cloaks. Keeping their faces down, they walked into the tent. Goblins jostled them on every side, trying to elbow their way to the front.

"Oh no," Rachel whispered. "Look!"

In the middle of the tent was a large circle of sawdust and a rickety old ladder. A tightrope wire was at the top of it, close beneath the roof of the tent. Rachel gasped and Kirsty groaned. Their old friend Queenie was standing on the platform at the top of the ladder with a green ribbon tangled around her wings. A goblin was beside her, clinging to the platform rail with all his strength.

"Please put your hands together for the guest of honour," boomed a voice.

The crowd of goblins clapped and parted, and then Jack Frost strode towards

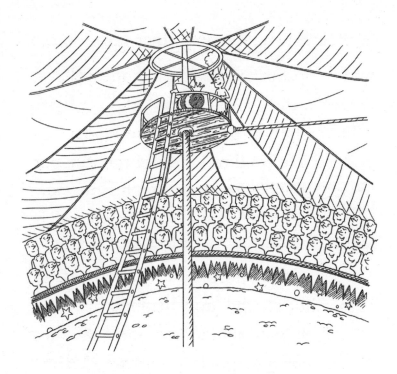

the middle of the tent. One lone goblin
blew a wobbly fanfare on a trumpet.
Rachel, Kirsty and Brianna were close
enough to reach out and touch Jack
Frost. They kept their heads down, hoping
that he wouldn't ask why they were
wearing cloaks.

"Pathetic," Jack Frost bellowed. "I even had to do my own introduction! Well, come on then. Get on with it!"

The goblin at the top of the ladder nodded. He tried to let go of the rail, but his legs wobbled and he clutched it again.

"I'm going to need some volunteers," he said in a weak voice.

Not a single green hand went up. Kirsty glanced at Rachel and Brianna.

"This is our chance," she said. "We have to pretend to be goblins until we reach the top or they will stop us. Climb, don't fly!"

Walking in single file, the fairies hurried to the ladder.

Chapter Fifteen
Saving the Bees

"Oh my goodness," said Brianna as she started to climb. "I think flying is much easier than this!"

Kirsty and Rachel were not afraid of heights, but even they felt a little bit dizzy when they reached the top and looked down. The crowd below looked like tiny

green dots, except for the spiky
white-and-blue dot that was Jack Frost.

"I d-don't l-like th-this," said the goblin
clinging to the platform rail. "My l-legs
have g-gone all wibbly-wobbly."

"You can climb down," said Rachel.
"We'll look after Qu— I mean – the
bee."

"Oh, thank goodness," the goblin
exclaimed.

He started to clamber down, and a
grumbling rumble came from the crowd
below.

"Get on with it."

"Where's the show?"

Brianna untied the green ribbon, while
Rachel and Kirsty slipped their arms
around Queenie's neck and kissed the top
of her furry head.

"Hello, old friend," said Kirsty.

"We're here to rescue you," Rachel added.

Queenie buzzed gratefully.

"Stop!" Jack Frost howled.

The three fairies threw off their cloaks.

"We won't stop," Kirsty declared bravely. "It's wrong to make an animal do scary tricks. Queenie should be free."

"It's that pesky bee fairy again!" Jack Frost roared.

He raced to the ladder and started to climb.

"I have all my magical objects back, thanks to Rachel and Kirsty," said Brianna. "Now there is only one thing left to do – escape!"

She pointed her wand at the tent roof, and the black-and-yellow stripes melted away.

"Come on, Queenie," said Rachel.

The three fairies and the bee zoomed up through the hole in the roof. Jack Frost's angry shouts faded away behind them. Soon, the grey sky became blue and the sun beat down on them. They landed in Brianna's bee garden and their cloaks disappeared with a twirl.

"Now my open morning can go ahead," said Brianna. "I even have my wonderful guest of honour back where she belongs. Thank you, my amazing friends."

"It was our pleasure to help," said Rachel.

Queenie nuzzled against them, giving her thanks too.

"You have your own event to get back to," Brianna went on. "I think you'll find that things are a lot easier now that my magical objects are safe again. Goodbye, and good luck. Remember to always be kind to bees!"

"We will!" Rachel and Kirsty promised. "Goodbye, Brianna! Goodbye, Queenie!"

They heard a soft buzz as they were whisked up in a flurry of fairy dust. Blinking, they whizzed back through the iron spirals of the Tippington peace garden gates.

"We're human again," said Rachel, reaching over her shoulder to check if she still had wings.

"What an adventure!" said Kirsty.

"We're about to have another one," Rachel went on. "Look!"

There was a queue of people outside the gates, all holding Bee Kind leaflets.

"Yes!" Kirsty cheered. "Now that Brianna has her magical objects back, people care about bees again."

"I can't wait," said Rachel. "Let's start saving the bees!"

The End

Now it's time for Kirsty and Rachel to help ...

Konnie the Christmas Cracker Fairy

Read on for a sneak peek ...

"This is going to be great," said Kirsty Tate, smiling at her best friend, Rachel Walker, as they arrived at the Tippington Community Centre.

It was almost Christmas, and Kirsty was staying with Rachel for the weekend. They had tied tinsel into their ponytails, and were feeling fizzy with Christmas excitement.

"It's going to be fun to learn how to make crackers," said Rachel. "Mum said that she'd come and buy some for

Christmas Day."

All the crackers were going to be sold at the Tippington Community Centre Christmas Fair that afternoon.

"What will happen to the money we raise at the fair?" Kirsty asked.

"Fingers crossed there will be enough to give the community centre a new coat of paint," said Rachel. "It looks a bit tatty!"

They looked up at the building. It was faded and weatherbeaten, and the old paint was starting to peel off. The only thing that made it jolly was the banner hanging above the door, held up with glittering threads of tinsel:

Eco Cracker Workshop Today!

Inside, the room was sparkling with garlands of tinsel. Wooden tables were arranged in a big square and covered with long, red cloths. There were different craft materials on each table. The girls could see bowls filled with cardboard tubes, colourful paper hats, red ribbon and stripy red-and-white string. Lots of people were already bustling around the tables.

A woman hurried towards them, smiling. She had soft, blonde hair that fluffed out around her head like a golden cloud, and a colourful dress with big, orange flowers all over it.

"Welcome!" she exclaimed. "I'm Susie, and I'm running the cracker workshop. What are your names?"

"I'm Rachel and this is Kirsty," said Rachel, smiling back at her.

Susie took a roll of labels and a felt-tip pen from the nearest table. In a few strokes, she had written their names in beautiful looped writing, decorated with tiny flowers and leaves.

"These look amazing," said Kirsty as she stuck the label to her T-shirt. "Thank you."

Susie led them over to a table where sheets of paper were stacked up in neat piles, covered in printed black writing.

"These are jokes," she said. "I printed them out on my computer at home. All we need to do now is cut each one out, ready to go into the crackers. That's your first job. Just grab a joke sheet and get snipping."

"Will we put the strips of paper into the crackers?" said Kirsty.

"Yes, later," said Susie. "First, we have to get the jokes, hats and eco-friendly gifts ready. Then I'll show everyone how to make the crackers. We're going to have lots of fun being super creative – with no plastic to harm the planet."

Eagerly, Rachel and Kirsty each picked up a sheet.

"Who delivers Christmas presents to cats?" Rachel read out. "Wrap."

She and Kirsty shared a puzzled look.

"I don't get it," said Kirsty.

"Try one from your sheet," said Rachel.

"What do Santa's little helpers learn at school?" Kirsty read aloud. "A puddle."

"That doesn't make sense," said Rachel.

She ran her finger down the jokes on her sheet and shook her head.

"Not a single one of these jokes is funny," she said. "Something has gone wrong!"

When Rachel and Kirsty told Susie about the jokes, her big smile faded.

"I can't understand how they have been muddled up," she said. "I must have done something wrong when I printed them. Well done for noticing, girls. Oh dear, it's going to take ages to match each joke to the right answer."

"We can do it," said Rachel in a confident voice. "Don't worry."

"I'll go and tell the other helpers," said Susie.

She hurried over to the next table and Kirsty looked at the pile of joke sheets.

"Oh my goodness, this is a big job," she said. "I wish we had a fairy to help us."

The girls exchanged a little smile, thinking about the marvellous secret that they shared. Since they had met on Rainspell Island, they had been on countless magical adventures with their fairy friends. Sometimes they had even become fairies themselves.

"Yes," said Rachel with a laugh. "Fairy magic would do this job in a twinkling."

Read **Konnie the Christmas Cracker Fairy** to find out what adventures are in store for Kirsty and Rachel!

RAINBOW magic

Calling all parents, carers and teachers!
The Rainbow Magic fairies are here to help
your child enter the magical world of reading.
Whatever reading stage they are at, there's
a Rainbow Magic book for everyone!
Here is Lydia the Reading Fairy's guide to
supporting your child's journey at all levels.

Starting Out

Our Rainbow Magic Beginner Readers are perfect for first-time readers who are just beginning to develop reading skills and confidence. Approved by teachers, they contain a full range of educational levelling, as well as lively full-colour illustrations.

1

Developing Readers

Rainbow Magic Early Readers contain longer stories and wider vocabulary for building stamina and growing confidence. These are adaptations of our most popular Rainbow Magic stories, specially developed for younger readers in conjunction with an Early Years reading consultant, with full-colour illustrations.

2

Going Solo

The Rainbow Magic chapter books – a mixture of series and one-off specials – contain accessible writing to encourage your child to venture into reading independently. These highly collectible and much-loved magical stories inspire a love of reading to last a lifetime.

3

www.rainbowmagicbooks.co.uk

"Rainbow Magic got my daughter reading chapter books. Great sparkly covers, cute fairies and traditional stories full of magic that she found impossible to put down" – Mother of Edie (6 years)

"Florence LOVES the Rainbow Magic books. She really enjoys reading now" – Mother of Florence (6 years)

Read along the Reading Rainbow!

Well done – you have completed the book!

This book was worth 2 stars.

See how far you have climbed on the Reading Rainbow opposite.
The more books you read, the more stars you can colour in
and the closer you will be to becoming a Royal Fairy!

Do you want to print your own Reading Rainbow?

1) Go to the Rainbow Magic website

2) Download and print out the poster

3) Colour in a star for every book you finish
and climb the Reading Rainbow

4) For every step up the rainbow,
you can download your very own certificate

There's all this and lots more at
rainbowmagicbooks.co.uk

You'll find activities, stories, a special newsletter
AND you can search for the fairy with your name!